NESSA'S STORY

Books by Nancy Luenn and Neil Waldman

Nessa's Fish
Mother Earth
Nessa's Story

NESSA'S STORY

by Nancy Luenn

Illustrated by Neil Waldman

Text copyright © 1994 by Nancy Luenn
Illustrations copyright © 1994 by Neil Waldman

All rights reserved. No part of this book may be reproduced
or transmitted in any form or by any means, electronic
or mechanical, including photocopying, recording, or by any
information storage and retrieval system, without permission
in writing from the Publisher.

This edition is reprinted by arrangement with Atheneum Books
For Young Readers, Simon & Schuster
Children's Publishing Division.
**Text copyright © 1994 by Nancy Luenn, illustrations
copyright © 1994 by Neil Waldman.
All rights reserved.**

First edition

10 9 8 7 6 5 4
The text of this book is set in Optima.
The illustrations are rendered in watercolor.

Library of Congress Cataloging-in-Publication Data
Luenn, Nancy.
Nessa's story / by Nancy Luenn; illustrated by Neil Waldman.—
1st ed.
p.   cm.
Summary: A young Inuit girl, who wishes she had something to
contribute when the adults tell their stories in the gathering
place, encounters the story of a lifetime when she finds a giant egg
one day and is able to see what it hatches.

1. Eskimos—Juvenile fiction. [1. Eskimos—Fiction. 2. Indians
of North America—Fiction.] I. Waldman, Neil, ill. II. Title.
PZ7.L9766Nf   1994
[E]—dc20   92-16984

For Suzanne
N. L.

*For Jessie Waldman, my mother,
who filled my first days with the light of love*
N. W.

All through the long winter, Nessa listened to her grandmother's stories. When her grandmother told stories in the gathering place, stories of claw-trolls and ten-legged bears and great shaggy *silaq,* everyone listened.

Nessa wanted a story of her own to tell.

She looked for her story all that winter and on through the spring.

Summer came. The tundra was noisy with birds.

"Nessa," said her grandmother, sitting up in the tent one morning. "This old woman is hungry for eggs."

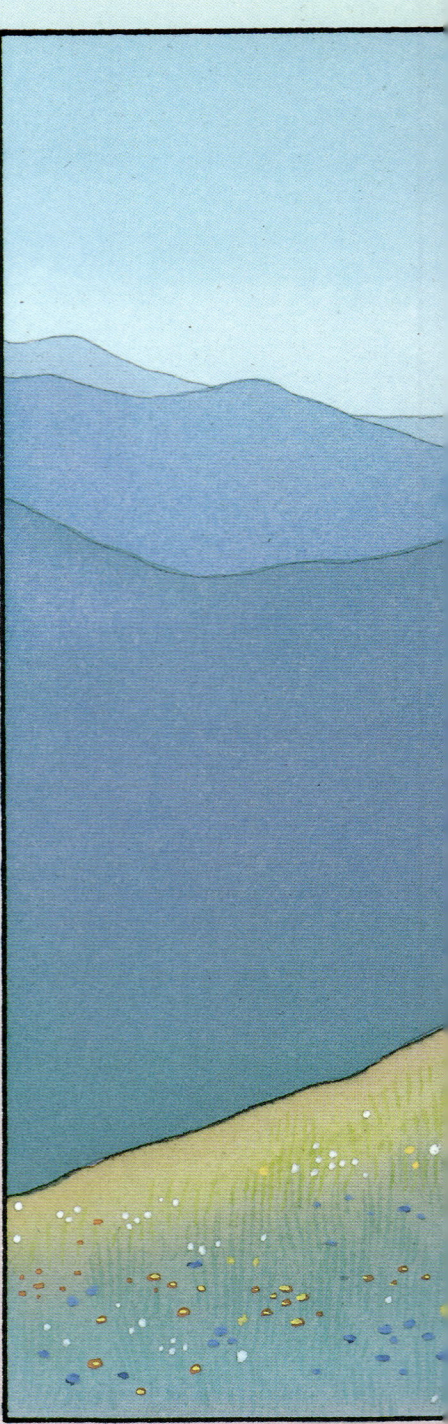

Nessa pulled on her sealskin boots. She took a skin bag and a pointed stick and set off to look for birds' eggs.

She walked across the tundra. She found a lemming's tunnel in the grass, the bones of a fox, and four spotted eggs.

Nessa put the eggs into her bag. Then she walked on, seeking something that might be her story.

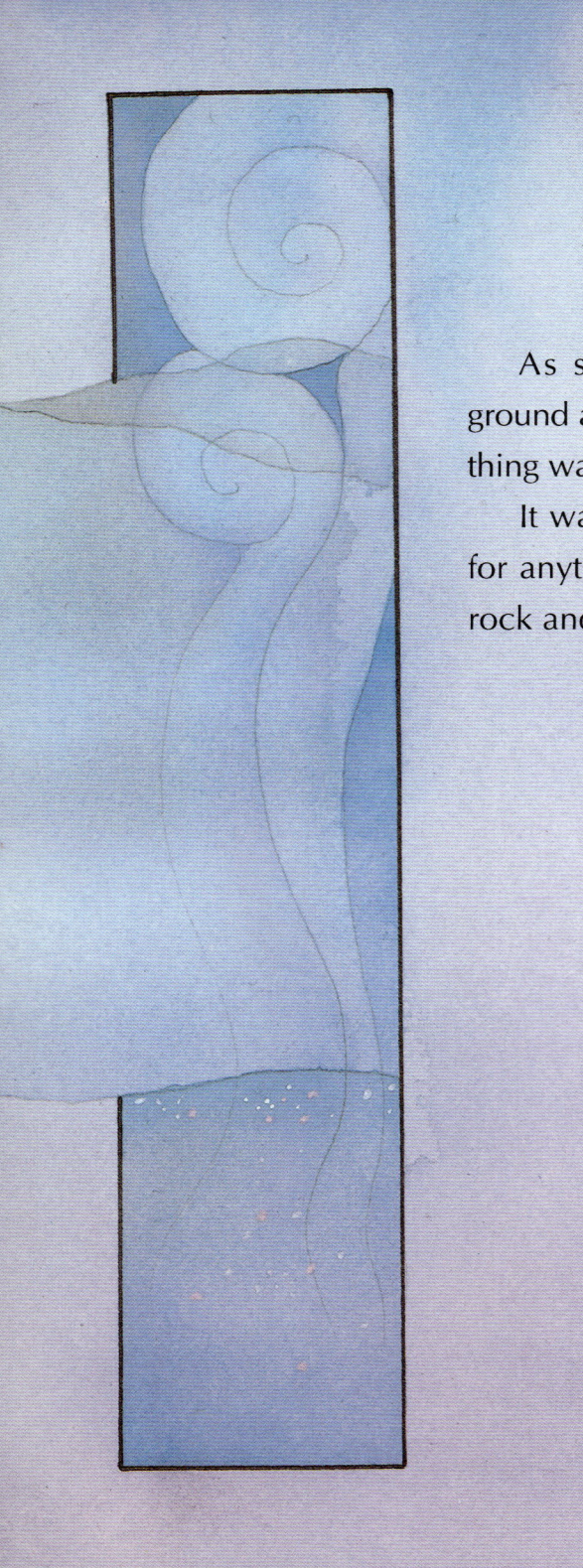

As she walked, fog rose from the ground and curled around her. Soon everything was gray.

It was so gray that it was hard to look for anything. She sat beside a large white rock and waited for the fog to clear.

Fog drifted past, making shapes in the air. She began to hear noises—sneezing and snorting and wuffling sounds. Nessa thought of bears. Then she thought of claw-trolls.

Nessa shivered. She looked for something else to think about. At her back, the rock was warm. . . .

Maybe, she thought, it isn't a rock. Maybe it's an egg.

While she waited for the fog to clear, she tried to imagine what might be inside.

Nessa heard a tapping sound. She jumped up and grabbed her stick, ready to defend her egg.

Not far away, a caribou raised its head and snorted. Caribou were grazing all around her. They didn't sense any danger.
Tap! Tap-tap.

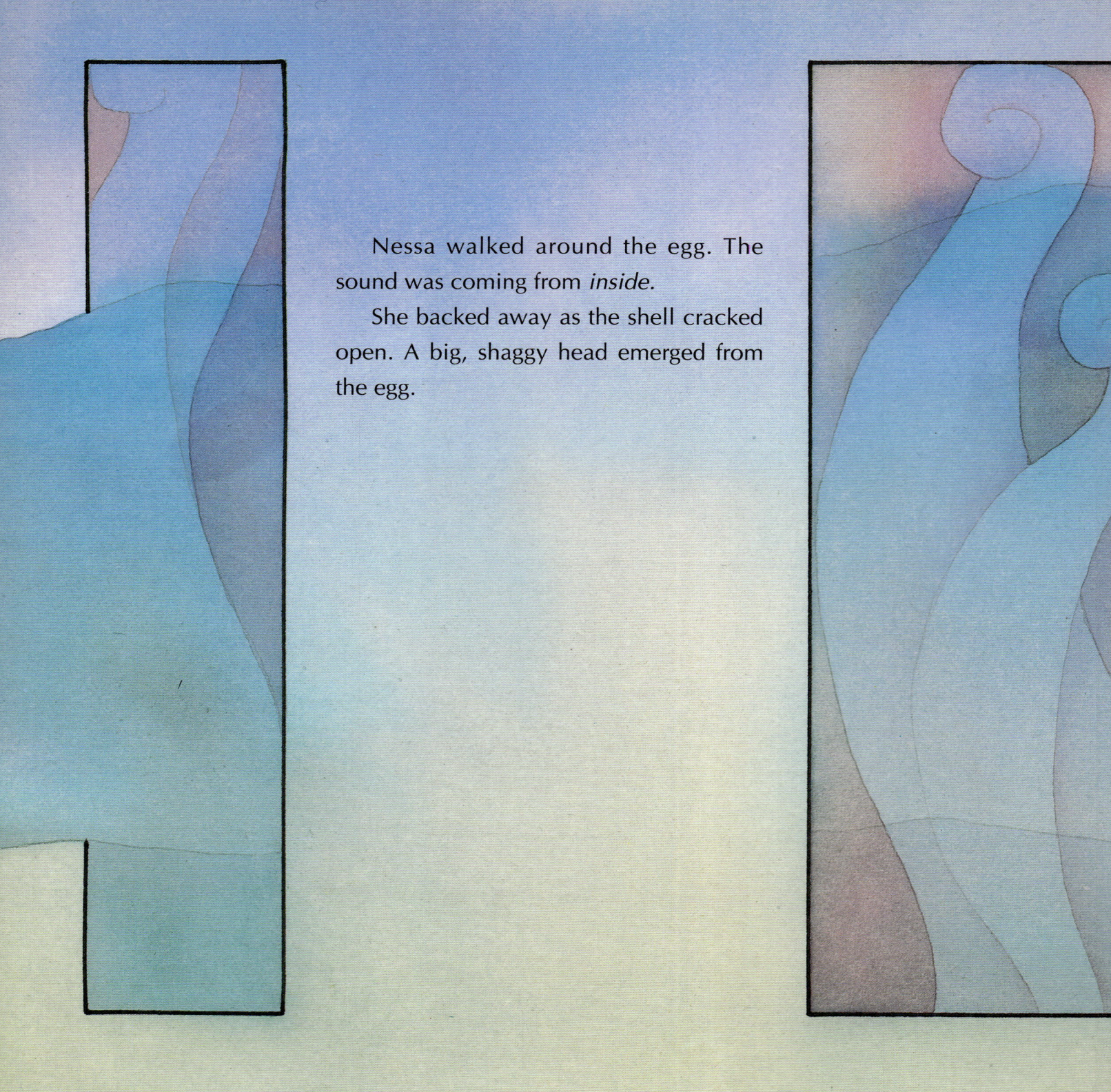

Nessa walked around the egg. The sound was coming from *inside*.

She backed away as the shell cracked open. A big, shaggy head emerged from the egg.

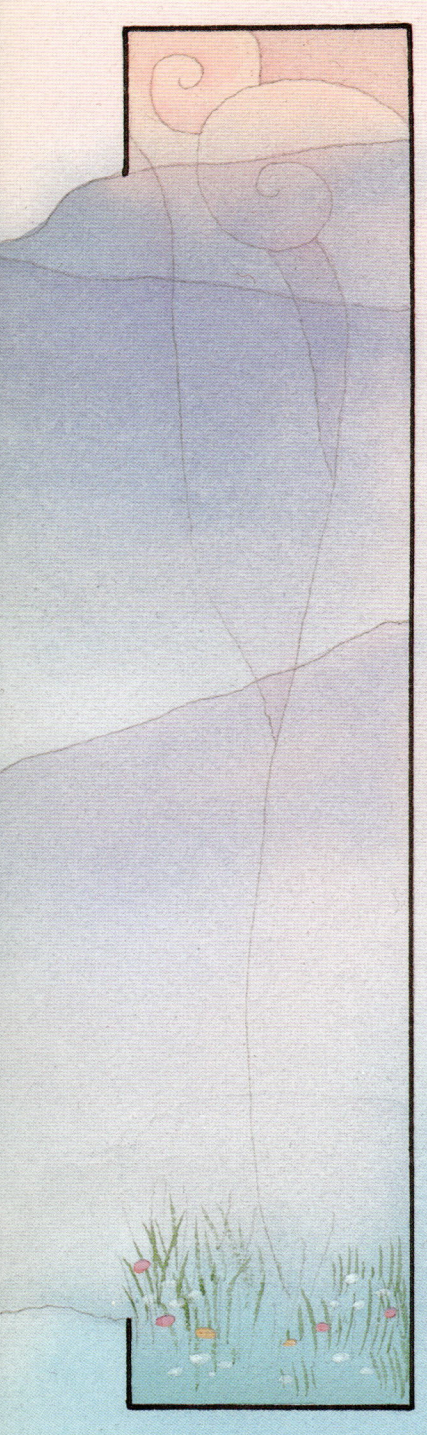

Out hatched the strangest animal she had ever seen. It had a large snout, short white tusks, and legs as strong as tent poles.

I wonder what it is? thought Nessa. Maybe it's a *silaq*!

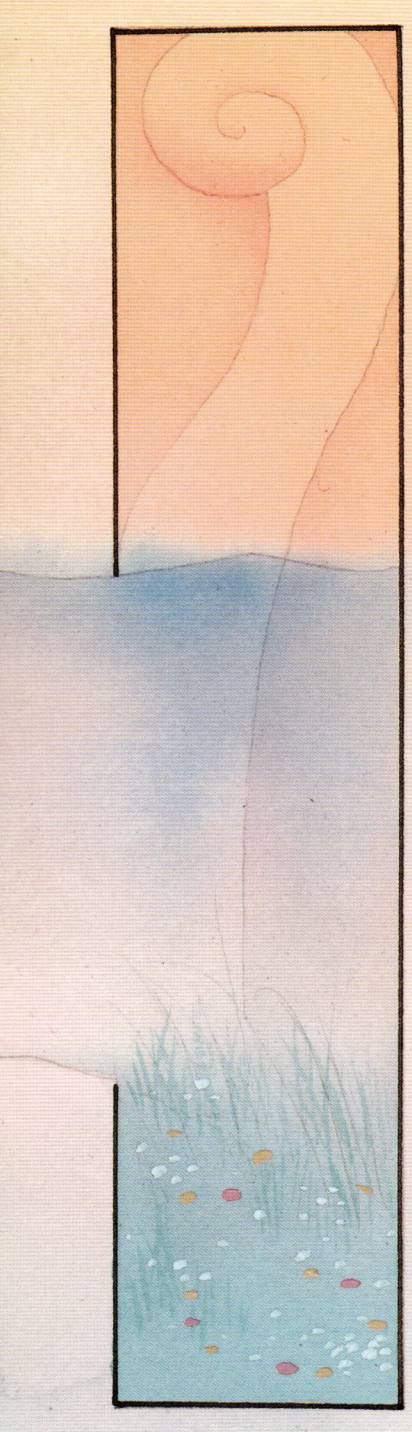

No one in camp, not even her grandmother, had ever seen an animal like this one.

The *silaq* pulled up a trunkful of grass and tucked the grass into its mouth. It chewed slowly, watching Nessa with one big, dark eye. She stared back at it, amazed.

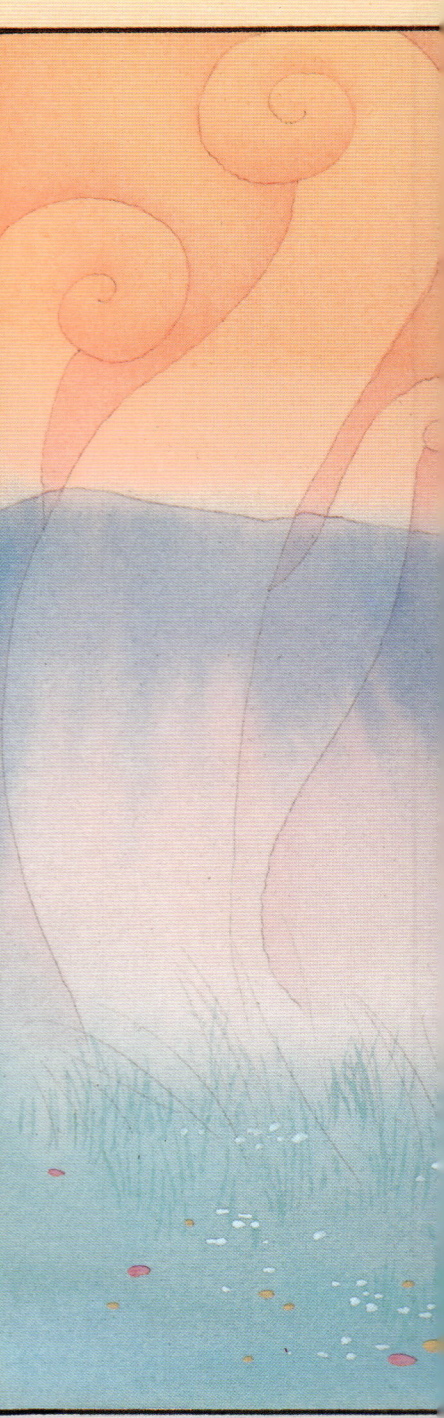

Just then, the sun came gleaming through the fog. Quick as a lemming, the *silaq* burrowed into the earth.

Nessa watched it disappear. She couldn't wait to tell her grandmother.

She made her way back through the lifting fog, past an empty nest, the bones of a fox, and a lemming's tunnel in the grass.

Nessa ran to her grandmother's arms and gave her the eggs.

"Have you been gathering eggs all day long?" asked her grandmother.

"I found a *giant* egg," said Nessa. "Listen!"

Now Nessa had a story of her own to tell.

And everyone listened.

Author's Note

This story was inspired by a legendary animal the Inuit (Eskimos) call *silaq* or *kilivfak*. Arctic cultures have various legends about a huge, shaggy animal that comes out of the earth. The people of Siberia said it lived underground and would die if touched by sunlight. The Eskimos of northern Alaska said the *kilivfak* could burrow into the earth like a giant mole. And the Inuit of the Canadian Arctic said the *silaq* hatched from a large white egg. Perhaps these legends recall a time when woolly mammoths roamed the Arctic tundra.